For Katy, Kirsty, Alex and Amy Lister,
and for the pupils and staff of Nakirungu Primary
and Secondary Schools, Uganda – *E.D.*

First published in Great Britain and in the USA in 2013 by
Frances Lincoln Children's Books, 74-77 White Lion Street,
London N1 9PF
www.frances-lincoln.com

A catalogue record for this book is available from the British Library.

ISBN 978-1-84780-338-2

Illustrated with watercolour and inks

Set in Cantoria MT

Printed in China

3 5 7 9 8 6 4 2

OFF TO
MARKET

Elizabeth Dale  Illustrated by **Erika Pal**

F
FRANCES LINCOLN
CHILDREN'S BOOKS

Here is the bus off to market today,
Shiny and bright as it starts on its way,
With Joe, the young driver, smiling with pride,
When everyone stops him to get on and ride.

On climb the mummies, their children and toys,
Hurry up, ladies, hop inside, boys!
Keb helps them on, oh isn't this fun!
Toot! Toot! Off we go, the journey's begun.

Next stop, **more families** are wanting a ride.
Can they fit in? Well, they all pile inside,
Carrying melons and boxes and coats,
Baskets and chickens and, goodness – two goats!

The bus **STOPS** again – oh dear, what a queue,
All wanting to ride on the market bus, too.
Some climb on the roof, and more squash inside,
If only the bus had been made twice as wide!

Here is the bus going ever so slow,
They shouldn't take more, but poor Joe can't say no!
With their rugs and their veggies, they squish and they squeeze,
Now everyone's sitting on somebody's knees!

Apart from young Keb, who is sitting on top
Of a goat and two sheep who all wriggle non-stop
As he jiggles around, and they nibble his shoe.
He laughs, for up there he has got the best view!

But the hill is so steep that the bus slows right down,
And then as it **STOPS** all the passengers frown.
"I'm sorry, the bus is too heavy," calls Joe.
"Some people must leave it before we can go."

The passengers shout, "But we can't get off here.
We're going to market, **we're not even near**!"
"But someone must leave – who will do it?" asks Joe.
"If you all stay on board, then no one can go."

"Well, I cannot walk," says a man with a shrug,
"I've six dozen eggs, twenty loaves and a jug."
A poor lady cries, "I've four geese and my bed,
I really can't carry them **all** on my head!"

And everyone else says they're laden down, too.
Joe scratches his head, what is he to do?
And then, from the back, there comes a faint shout,
"I'll get off," cries Keb, "if you **all** let me out!"

So up gets the woman with both of her goats,
The man who is selling a huge pile of coats,
The lady with chickens all making a fuss,
Till **finally** Keb makes his way off the bus.

Then Joe starts the engine – or rather, he tries,
But it splutters and coughs and then finally dies.
"I'll give you a push!" Keb calls out to Joe.
Joe smiles – little Keb could not make the bus go!

But before all the others can climb on again,
Keb pushes and **pushes** and **shoves** hard and then
The bus moves an inch, well now, what do you know?
It's over the hill, and is starting to go. . .

"Climb on quickly," calls Joe, "if you still want a ride!"
And everyone scrambles to get back inside –
The lady with chicks and the man with the coats,
The rug man, the woman with both of her goats.

Then Keb quickly gives one more **push** from the back
And jumps on the bus as it speeds down the track.
Quicker and quicker! The bus goes so fast,
Bushes and houses and rivers flash past.

And everyone laughs – they haven't a care,
They'll get to the market and have time to spare.
So they all give a **cheer** and a **great big hooray**
For kind little Keb who's shown them that day
That everyone's useful, no matter how small,
For a big heart will make you at least ten feet tall!

Then the passengers say they will buy Keb a treat.
Does he choose a new hat, something yummy to eat?
Or a ball and a bat or a shiny blue boat?
No, the one thing he wants most of all is a. . .

goat!

And to round off a day that's the best there could be,
Joe says Keb can ride all the way home for **free!**